A little boy asks, *How does a cow go to sleep—tell me how?* And his father replies, *A cow lies down in the soft sweet hay, In a cozy barn at the end of the day.*

In this tender bedtime story each of the animals in the barnyard prepares for the night: The duck tucks his head right under his wing, the pig curls up with family and friends, the horse stands up while he's fast asleep, and the hen fluffs her feathers and sits on her nest.

Enchanting illustrations by Juan Wijngaard capture the warm and loving answers a father gives to his young son as they too prepare for the night.

Wendy Cheyette Lewison

has written many books for young children, including *Mud!,* and several pop-up and activity books. *Going to Sleep on the Farm* is her first book for Dial. Ms. Lewison lives in Larchmont, New York.

Juan Wijngaard

was born in Argentina but moved to Holland as a boy, and subsequently lived in England, where he studied art at the Royal College of Art. He has won several major awards for his illustrations, including the 1985 Kate Greenaway Medal for *Sir Gawain and the Loathly Lady.* Mr. Wijngaard now lives in Santa Monica, California, with his family.

Wendy Cheyette Lewison

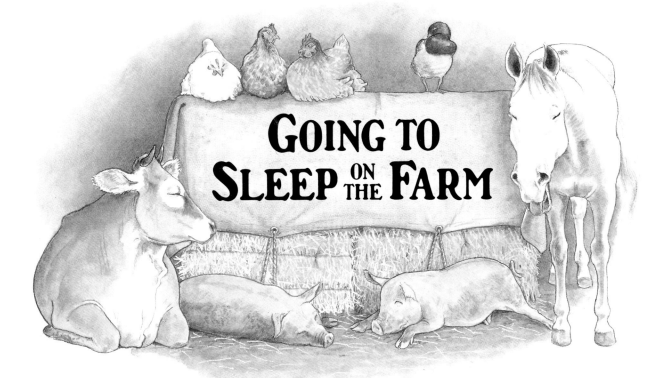

GOING TO
SLEEP ON THE FARM

pictures by Juan Wijngaard

Dial Books for Young Readers

New York

For Bea and Josh Cheyette, my mother and father,
who sang me to sleep. W.C.L.

To Patrick J.W.

Published by arrangement with Dial Books for Young Readers
A Division of Penguin Books USA Inc.

Text copyright © 1992 by Wendy Cheyette Lewison
Pictures copyright © 1992 by Juan Wijngaard
All rights reserved
Designed by Atha Tehon
Printed in Belgium
First Edition
3 5 7 9 10 8 6 4

Library of Congress Cataloging in Publication Data
Lewison, Wendy Cheyette. Going to sleep on the farm/
by Wendy Cheyette Lewison ; pictures by Juan Wijngaard.

p. cm.

Summary: A father describes for his son how each animal
on the farm goes to sleep.
ISBN: 0-8037-1096-8.—ISBN 0-8037-1097-6 (lib. ed.)
[1. Domestic animals—Fiction. 2. Sleep—Fiction 3. Bedtime—Fiction.
4. Stories in rhyme.] I. Wijngaard, Juan, ill. II. Title.
PZ8.3.L592Go 1992 [E]—dc20 91-3737 CIP AC

The art for this book was prepared by using watercolors.
It was then color-separated and reproduced
in red, yellow, blue, and black halftones.

How does a cow go to sleep—tell me how?
How does a cow go to sleep?

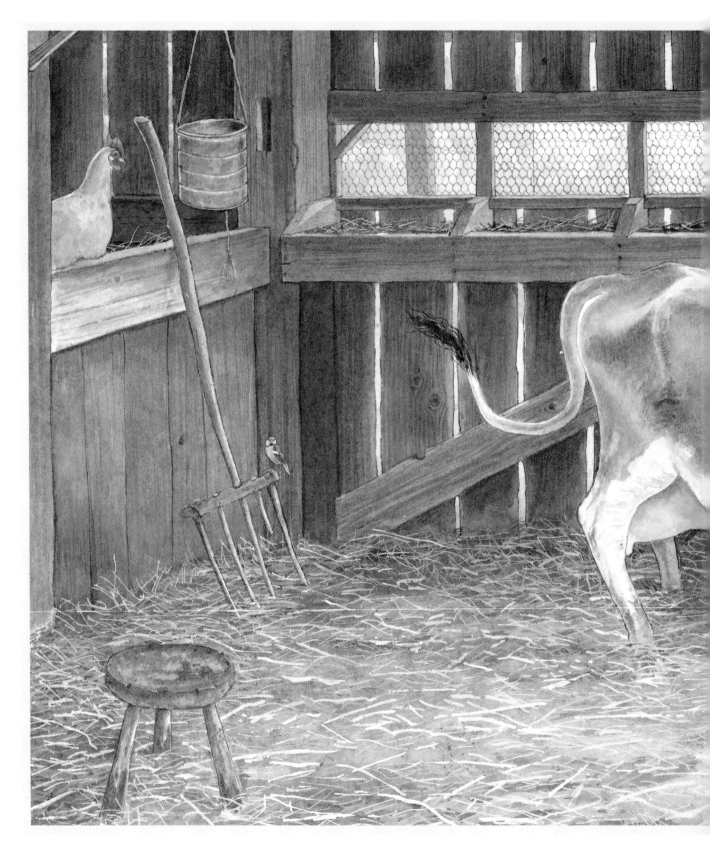

A cow lies down in the soft, sweet hay,

in a cozy barn, at the end of day.

And that's how a cow goes to sleep—Moo-moo.
That's how a cow goes to sleep.

How does a duck go to sleep—tell me how?
How does a duck go to sleep?

A duck tucks his bill right under his wing,

and doesn't worry about a thing.

And that's how a duck goes to sleep—Quack, quack.
That's how a duck goes to sleep.

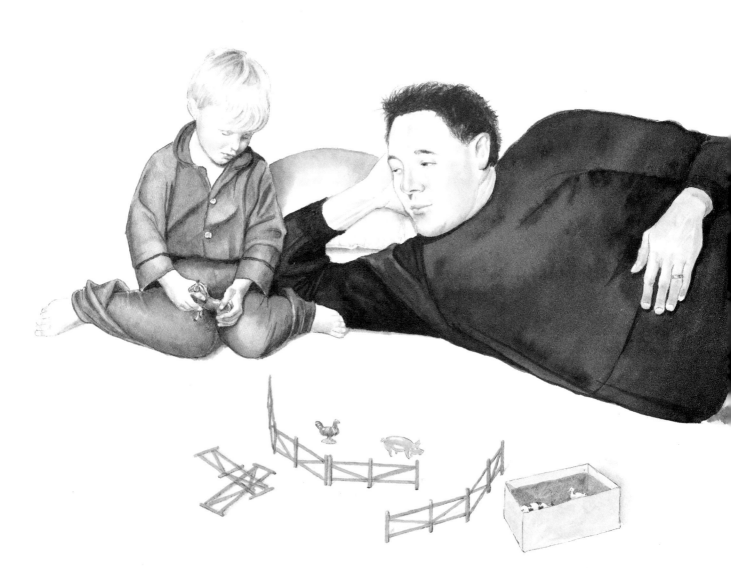

How does a horse go to sleep—tell me how?
How does a horse go to sleep?

A horse, of course, stands up all night,

while he's fast asleep, with his eyes shut tight.

And that's how a horse goes to sleep—Neighh-h-h.
That's how a horse goes to sleep.

How does a pig go to sleep—tell me how?
How does a pig go to sleep?

A pig curls up with her family or friends.

Where one pig starts, another pig ends.

And that's how a pig goes to sleep—Oink, oink.
That's how a pig goes to sleep.

How does a hen go to sleep—tell me how?
How does a hen go to sleep?

A hen fluffs her feathers so they look their best,

and sits on her eggs, all warm in her nest.

And that's how a hen goes to sleep—Cluck, cluck.
That's how a hen goes to sleep.

How do you go to sleep—tell me how?
How do you go to sleep?

You snuggle down in your nice warm bed,
And sleepy dreams soon fill your head.

And that's how you go to sleep—Shh-h-h.
That's how you go to sleep.